HARRY and
THE SEA SERPENT

HARRY and THE SEA SERPENT

written and illustrated
by Gahan
Wilson

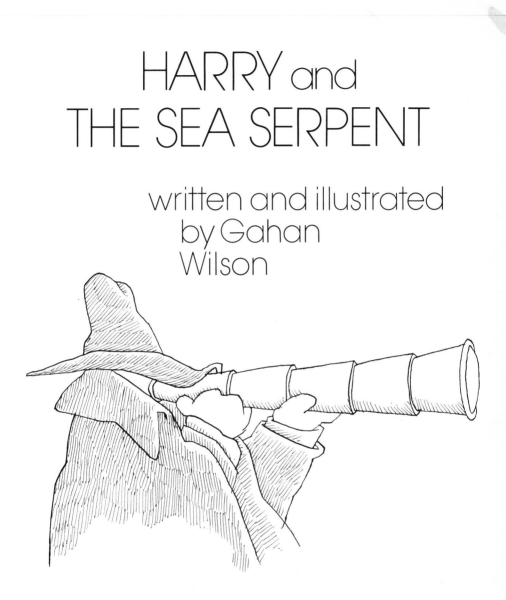

Charles Scribner's Sons   New York

This one is for
Clare and Kate Ellis
(because they liked
the first one)

1 3 5 7 9 11 13 15 17 19 MD/C 20 18 16 14 12 10 8 6 4 2

Printed in the United States of America
Library of Congress Catalog Card Number 75-35008
ISBN 0-684-14584-7

Contents

Map of Northeastern Bearmania 6–7

one   A Coded Command   9

two   A View of the Jo-Anne-Mae   16

three   A Plague of Sea Tulips   24

four   Professor Waldo   34

five   Green Blurs   44

six   A Rough Voyage   55

seven   Left Bear Paw Island   64

eight   A Run Along the Water   73

nine   A Surprise Visitor   83

ten   The Sighting   92

eleven   The Serpent Watchers   100

twelve   The Chase   108

thirteen Everybody Has a Party   121

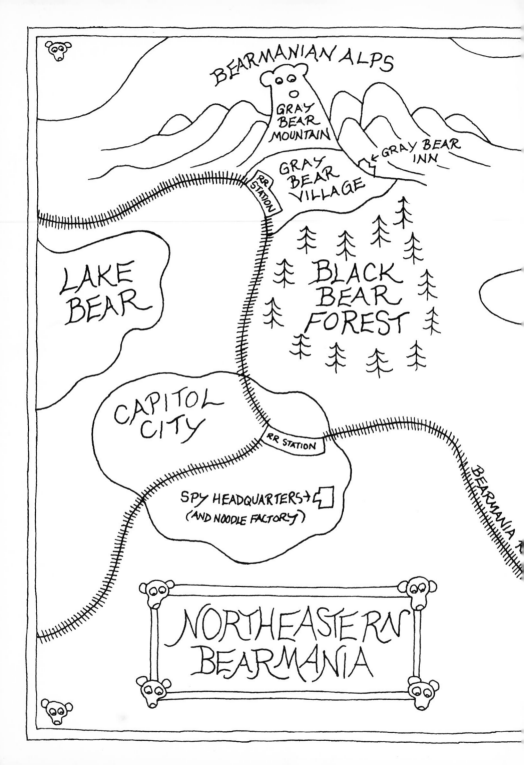

He was on vacation.

one A Coded Command

The sun was bright, the sea sparkled, and Harry the fat bear spy walked happily along the beach at Beartown-on-the-Sea. He was on vacation, his first in years, and he had enjoyed three full days of doing nothing but wade, gather interesting shells into his sand bucket, sleep, and eat nice things.

Of course he wore his regulation spy hat, he was never without that, but also, to show he was on vacation, he wore a bright yellow and orange striped bathing suit. At first he had been timid about wearing it, it was very different from his usual black outfit, but now he loved it and was proud of being so colorful a bear.

Soon, and Harry smacked his lips at the thought, it would be lunchtime and he would be able to enjoy more of the pastry spread with strawberry jam and thick, sweet cream which was the local specialty here at Beartown-on-the-Sea. His mouth watered and his stomach rumbled and he ate a macaroon to tide him over.

Harry looked down the beach, where his fellow spy and

partner, Fred, otherwise known as Agent Ten Zero Zero Three, sat hunched and frowning, peering intently at a bit of paper in his hands. Harry, otherwise known as Agent Three Five Zero small case *b*, shook his head and sighed. Poor Fred didn't seem to be enjoying the vacation at all. The whole idea of sitting around doing nothing in particular seemed to make him even more nervous and fretful than usual. If anything, the frown lines on his forehead had deepened these last few days. As Harry drew closer

"Why can't anybody do anything right?"

he could hear the thin bear muttering to himself peevishly.

"It doesn't make sense!" he said through clenched teeth. "None at all! Oh, why can't anybody do anything *right?*"

"What's wrong, Fred?" asked Harry.

"*This* is!" said Fred, waving the paper. "It's a message from the Spy Master. Coded, and as usual, all botched up!"

"Well, we always end up making sense out of his messages, Fred," said Harry. "More or less."

Harry took the paper and read the message as decoded by Fred and printed in his neat hand:

INVESTIGATE INVESTIGATE GALOSHES STOP CONTACT COMMODORE SOUNDS LIKE HOORAY TEA WHO? STOP STOP STOP

Harry pursed his lips and cleared his throat.

"Well, it *is* pretty bad," he admitted. "But that first thing, the business of his saying 'investigate' twice, well you know he does those unintentional repeats all the time."

"I do," growled the thin bear.

"Yes," continued Harry. "However, this thing with 'galoshes,' now, I confess that's got me somewhat confused. Er, could you let me have a peek at the code book, Fred? And the original message?"

"I wish just once things would go smoothly," said Fred, handing Harry the bulky *Official Bearmanian Spy Code and Foreign Language Phrase Book* and the coded message written in the Spy Master's hectic penmanship. Harry read the message carefully, turning the paper this way and that:

Dear Harry and Fred
Hope you are having a nice
vacation but now it is over.
asparagus.
asparagus.
paisley   Uncle Jules
slipper eskimo five.
paisley machinery nose
paisley
paisley
Sincerely
the S.M.

Harry shook his head, not for the first time, over the secret code used by the Bearmanian Spy Department. You were supposed to be able to use it to write ordinary-looking letters which would send secret messages without anybody suspecting a thing, but Harry could not imagine anyone in his right mind composing such a letter, nor anyone else thinking it was anything but a bunch of funny business. He decided it was just as well such things were left to wiser heads than his own. They probably knew what they were doing up at the top. At least he hoped so.

"Alright, then," said Harry. "About this 'galoshes.' In the code book it stands for 'Uncle Jules,' so let's check the other 'Uncles' and see if we can't come across something that makes a little more sense."

Harry went through the book until he came to a large section labeled *UNCLES* and he turned the pages listing the names of various Uncles and what they actually stood for in secret code until he came to the top of page 564:

Uncle Ichabod *actually means* "I'll be waiting for you"
Uncle Igan *actually means* "You'll be waiting for me"
Uncle Igor *actually means* "Parsnips"

Uncle Ivan *actually means* "Sea Serpent"
Uncle Jerome *actually means* "Pastry"
Uncle Jules *actually means* "Galoshes"
Uncle Karl *actually means* "Don't call me Wednesday"

Harry raised his eyebrows and smiled.

"Well, that's it," he said, a little smugly.

"What's it?" asked Fred.

Harry put his finger on a word in the list and turned the book so that Fred could read it.

"You see?" asked Harry. "He put down the wrong Uncle. He meant to say 'investigate pastry,' which is, of course, by far the most interesting thing there is to investigate here in Beartown-on-the-Sea."

Fred squinted at the list.

"You sure he didn't mean 'sea serpent'?"

Harry only chuckled and raised his eyebrows a little higher.

"Well, I just don't see what a Commodore would know about pastry, is all," said Fred. "A Commodore being a kind of a sailor, as I understand. Even if his name does sound like Hooray Tea Who."

"The thing that puzzles me," said Harry, thoughtfully

"He put down the wrong Uncle."

closing the book, "is where we should go to contact the Commodore."

"There's a Navy base here at Beartown-on-the-Sea, Harry," said Fred. "It strikes me that might be a good place to start looking for a sailor."

"Good thinking, Fred," said Harry, regarding his partner with affection and respect.

two A View of
the Jo-Anne-Mae

Harry and Fred changed into their official black spy outfits, now that they were on official business, and though Fred seemed downright relieved to have his long, mysterious cloak back on, Harry gave his bright yellow and orange bathing suit a wistful look before he folded it carefully and put it in a drawer with an affectionate pat.

The two bears hurried along the cobblestone streets, heading for the Navy base which was, sensibly, located on the water. It was at the southernmost part of town and consisted of a red brick storage building with sails flapping out of the windows on its top floor, another brick building next to it with flowerboxes on its windowsills and a pretty sign reading

SAILOR'S REST

over its front door, and three wooden piers reaching out into the water.

"Well, will you look at that!" said Harry, pointing, for moored at the end of one of the piers was a sailing ship painted at least sixty different colors and trimmed in gold.

16

Harry gave his suit a wistful look.

Harry and Fred went out along the pier to get a better look at the colorful ship and saw a small bear suspended on a plank hung with ropes from the ship's railing. The bear was busily painting a panel of the ship a brilliant lemon yellow. The panel next to it was emerald green, and

The small bear was busily painting.

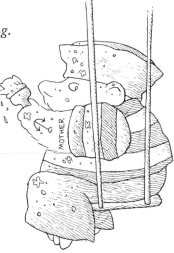

the one on the other side was a bold crimson. There did not seem to be any two parts of the ship painted in the same color, except for the golden trim which ran around all its edges and borders and covered the raised lettering on the bow and stern. Fred peered at the lettering, moving his lips as he read it.

"The *Jo-Anne-Mae*," murmured Fred.

"Why, it's one of the most cheerful boats I've ever seen," said Harry, looking with admiration at the brilliantly-hued craft.

"It is nice, isn't it?" said Fred a little grudgingly, since bright colors tended to make him nervous, even though he really did like them.

The small bear on the plank paused in his painting and looked down at the two spies. He wore a white cap, blue bell-bottomed pants, and a striped jersey, all of which were spotted and splashed with paint.

"I believe that's a sailor, Fred," whispered Harry, and then he called out: "Ahoy, aloft!"

"Hello," said the sailor, idly scratching at a spot of geranium pink on his nose. "Is there anything I can do for you?"

"Have you aboard a Commodore whose name sounds like Hooray Tea Who?" called out Harry.

The sailor paused and tugged thoughtfully at his left ear lobe, leaving a spot of yellow on it.

"I suppose you must mean Commodore Horatio," he answered.

"Aye aye," said Harry.

"The Commodore isn't on the boat right now, but he'll be back shortly if you'd care to wait."

Harry hesitated, then turned to Fred and asked: "Can you think of a nautical expression meaning 'thank you'?"

"Doesn't 'avast' mean something along those lines, Harry?"

"I don't believe it does, Fred."

"Well, then, I'd just say 'thank you' and let it go at that."

Harry did, and the sailor said he was perfectly welcome. Harry turned to leave but Fred took his arm, saying: "My goodness, Harry, will you look down here in the water!" Harry bent over and was startled to see that the *Jo-Anne-Mae* appeared to be sitting in a garden of lovely flowers.

"They seem to be some sort of water flowers," said Fred.

Harry smiled down at the pretty things as they bobbed gently below them. They were a delicate pink and white, and smelled faintly of cinnamon.

"My," said Harry, making a mental note to ask if he could pick some, "aren't they nice!"

Then the two bears walked idly about the Navy base, waiting for the return of the Commodore. Everything was neat and tidy—arranged, Harry supposed, according to Navy regulations.

As they passed the "Sailor's Rest," Harry smelled a waft of delicious fish chowder coming from one of the open windows and found that very reassuring. Then they came across a bulletin board mounted on an old anchor which had scraps of paper pinned and taped and tacked every which way to its surface. Some of them were notices of

"They seem to be some sort of water flowers, Harry."

boat sailings, some were lost and found notices, one bear was apparently having trouble selling a dory for he had crossed out and reduced his asking price for it a number of times, but right in the middle of the board, on by far the biggest paper of all, was the following:

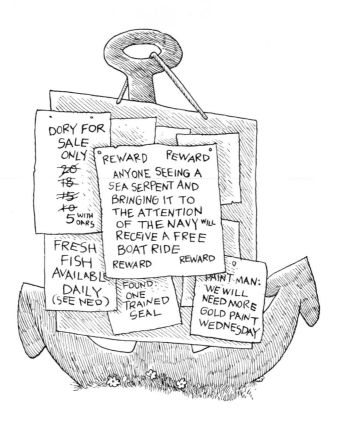

Harry and Fred looked at each other, and at almost the same instant they both remembered the words "sea serpent" in the Uncles list of the *Official Bearmanian Spy Code and Foreign Language Phrase Book.*

"Just as I thought, Harry. The Spy Master's secret message must have meant 'sea serpent,' " said Fred, excitedly. "We're supposed to investigate a sea serpent!"

"But there are no such things as sea serpents, Fred," said Harry.

"Oh yes there are!" boomed a voice right next to them, and when Harry and Fred turned to see who had spoken, they hadn't a doubt in the world they were looking at none other than Commodore Horatio of the Bearmanian Navy.

He was a large bear, fully as big as Harry, though nowhere near as fat. He wore a bright blue uniform covered with brass buttons and medals and gold braid, and he carried a huge copper telescope under one arm. He looked from Harry to Fred and back again, and then he smiled.

"And you must be the lads they have sent to help us catch the monster," he said.

"Oh yes there are!"

three A Plague of Sea Tulips

Sunlight sparkled off the sea and through Commodore Horatio's small-paned windows, dancing over the bright colors of the walls and furnishings of his cabin. It was as cheerful and pleasant a room as Harry had ever been in, but Harry was not even a tiny bit cheerful, nor was Fred. They were staring at a long parchment the Commodore had unrolled and spread before them on his map table.

"Bears have actually seen that?" asked Harry, pointing at the drawing on the parchment.

"They have," answered the Commodore. "And you can count among them Sailor Ned who's out there painting the *Jo-Anne-Mae*. Some have seen it not only once, but several times."

The drawing was unmistakably and without doubt one of a sea serpent. It coiled and writhed its way greenly all the way across the parchment, indicating that the real serpent must be a lot longer than anything Harry had ever heard of before. The drawing showed it to you sideways half above the water, and the other half submerged beneath. It seemed to swim in a series of loops with the upper parts of the loops showing above the water as a row of humps.

"Can you imagine," asked the Commodore, "what a menace to navigation a thing like that can be?"

"Very annoying, I'm sure," said Harry.

"We must get rid of it!" said the Commodore firmly.

The worst part about the drawing was the head. Harry stared at the long, yellow teeth, and the huge, glaring eyes,

It coiled and writhed its way across the parchment.

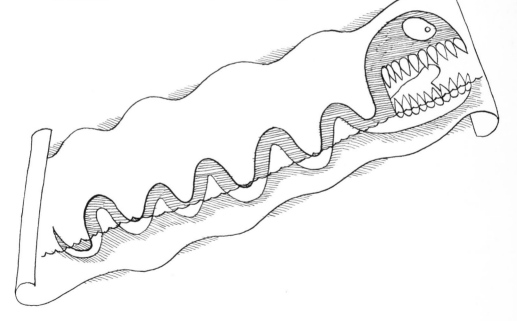

and he figured the mouth was plenty big enough to swallow a fat bear spy at a gulp, easy. Maybe two fat bear spies. Maybe three. He felt in his pockets for a macaroon and then decided he just didn't have the appetite.

"It's seen in the moonlight, mostly," said the Commodore, "swimming around Left Bear Paw Island, more than likely, but Sailor Ned saw it one twilight, and hard by the *Jo-Anne-Mae!*"

Commodore Horatio frowned darkly down at the drawing. "We would have got it then, mark me, were it not for those cursed sea tulips!" he growled.

"Sea tulips?" asked Harry.

"You don't know about that sea plague, then?" asked the Commodore. "I hate to be the one to tell you about the blasted things, but I will. Come take a look at this!"

He walked to the two large windows at the rear of his cabin and flung them open. Harry and Fred stood on either side of him and peered down. The Commodore was pointing angrily at the pretty water flowers they had admired before. The whole effect was really very pleasant, though Harry, realizing how the Commodore felt about sea tulips, decided it would be wiser not to say so.

"I'm told they were brought here by a little old lady bear

who traveled the world and got them someplace in the East. She grew the devilish things in a pond, but they spread, and have continued spreading, and have at present nearly brought coastal commerce in Bearmania to a halt."

"Come, take a look at this!"

The Commodore gripped the sill of his window tightly and glared down at the delicate flowers.

"Why, we thought they really looked kind of—" began Fred, but Harry, thinking quickly, cleared his throat noisily and interrupted his partner. "Terrible things!" he said loudly, and the Commodore nodded in agreement. "Really just awful!"

"But," said Fred, "we thought they were actually sort of—"

This time it was the Commodore who interrupted Fred.

"Do you know there are some people who think those things are pretty?" he asked. "Pretty! ! !"

"That's what I—" said Fred, but Harry, realizing Fred had somehow failed to understand that the Commodore would not like to hear nice things said about the sea tulips, gave his partner the secret signal which, in Bearmanian Spy Secret Signal Code, meant "Be quiet!"

"What's wrong?" asked Commodore Horatio, looking at Harry curiously. "Are you alright?"

"Oh, I'm fine," said Harry. "What makes you think anything's wrong?"

"Well, it's just the way you're suddenly standing," said the Commodore. "I mean with your left paw over your

*"What makes you think
anything is wrong?"*

mouth, and your left elbow up in the air, and your right arm making a circular motion over your head, and standing on your right foot with your left foot on your right knee, and all."

"Oh, that's nothing," said Fred. "That's a Bearmanian Spy Secret Sig—"

"Will you be *quiet*, Fred?" said Harry, who was beginning to feel rather out of sorts with his partner. "I'm sure the Commodore isn't interested in our Spy Exercises."

He turned to the Commodore, who still looked a bit puzzled. "They're just some simple muscular exercises to tone up the body. They require no equipment and can be done unobtrusively while the spy is on duty," Harry said quickly. Of course that was not true, but a spy must fib a little, now and then, to accomplish his dangerous work.

"Tell me, Commodore," said Harry, "just what is it about these terrible sea tulips that makes them so terrible?"

"Come on deck, lads," said the Commodore, "and I'll show you for yourselves."

They followed him up a brightly colored stairway until they found themselves outside, blinking in the sun. They walked along the railing, looking down over the side of the ship, as the Commodore talked.

"As you see, we are surrounded by the plaguey things in a bank up to ten feet wide, as is," and here he swung his paw in a great sweep to indicate the whole of Beartown-on-the-Sea. "And there's no telling if they will ever stop."

He took his copper telescope from under his arm and extended it about ten feet. He handed it to Harry, who nearly dropped it, having no idea how heavy it would be. Harry put the glass to his eye and saw that the Commodore was absolutely right: the whole harbor of Beartown-on-the-Sea and some of the coast on either side was lined with a good ten feet of thickly growing sea tulips.

"You cannot move a boat through them unless you chop

Harry could see that the Commodore was absolutely right.

your way with an ax or a machete," growled the Commodore. It was obvious the subject disturbed him deeply. "And there is no way, no way at *all* to get rid of them, and *that* is why they are so terrible."

"Ah!" said Harry.

"If it were not for *them*, lads, *we would have got the serpent when Sailor Ned spotted it that night!*"

"Oh?" said Harry.

"It was right there. He saw it rolling by," said the Commodore, glowering over the sea tulips, "impudent as you please, blast its scales!"

"Um!" said Harry.

"We made ready, hoisting anchor and raising sail, and in the normal course of events we would have caught the monster in a trice."

Harry was on the point of interjecting another comment, but the Commodore slammed his huge paw on the ship's railing, startling the fat bear into silence.

"But we couldn't move an inch, lads, due to those terrible sea tulips! They held our hull as firm as if their stalks and branches were made of steel cables, and we couldn't budge!"

Harry and Fred shook their heads sympathetically.

"I tell you I think I even heard the devilish monster give a muffled laugh!" said the Commodore. "And when it turned its awful face full in our direction, it stuck its huge yellow tongue out at us and then coiled its way to sea and out of sight!"

"Well," said Fred, moved by the Commodore's exciting story, "I can easily see why you're not particularly fond of those sea tulips!"

The naval officer clasped his paws behind his back and began to pace up and down the deck, shaking his head now and then, frowning and muttering to himself.

"Perhaps it would be a good idea to change the subject, Harry," whispered Fred.

"Not a bad idea, Fred," Harry whispered back. "He seems to have worked himself into a pretty bad mood."

"It's getting on to lunchtime, isn't it, Fred?" said Harry in a normal tone of voice. "Perhaps we'd best—"

But the Commodore broke in with an urgent request: "Hand me my telescope, lad!"

Harry did and the Commodore peered through it.

"What is he looking at, Harry?" asked Fred.

"I'm not sure, Fred," answered his friend. "But it's coming this way, and it's green!"

four Professor Waldo

Harry and Fred watched carefully as the green thing bobbed closer and closer to the *Jo-Anne-Mae*.

"I certainly hope that is what the bears around here have been mistaking for a sea serpent, Harry," said Fred.

"So do I, Fred," said Harry. "What I like best about it is that it doesn't seem to have any teeth."

"It doesn't even seem to have a mouth, Harry."

"That's right, Fred. And it's small. It seems to be about the size of a small, green tent."

"Actually, I think that's what it is, Harry. A small green tent."

"But what do you suppose a small, green tent is doing, floating toward us in the water?"

The Commodore slid his copper telescope shut to its ordinary size and turned to Harry and Fred.

"That is the floating, green tent of Professor Waldo, lads," said the Commodore. "He uses it to observe the serpent."

By now the tent had reached the outer edge of the sea

*"It's coming this way
and it's green!"*

tulips. A flap opened in the front of it and two rather
frail-looking bear paws emerged holding a large knife and
began to chop away at the flowers. Slowly the tent worked
its way to the side of the *Jo-Anne-Mae.*

"It does seem to be very hard to get through those
things," said Fred.

At last the tent bumped against the hull of the ship and,
after the front flap opened wider, a graying bear, wearing
thick glasses, peeked out and waved up at them. All three

bears waved back, and the graying bear disappeared momentarily again.

"The Professor has one of the greatest minds in Bearmania, lads," said the Commodore. "It is very fortunate for us here that he decided to retire to Beartown-on-the-Sea."

A graying bear peeked out and waved up at them.

Harry looked down at the tent with some awe.

"Is that *the* Professor Waldo?" he asked.

"None other!" said the Commodore, proudly.

"You mean *the* Professor Waldo?" asked Fred.

"The very one!"

Harry and Fred looked down at the little tent bobbing beneath them with excited interest. They had heard of Professor Waldo since they were very small bears, and Harry remembered a whole week in his high school physics class spent on nothing but the discoveries and inventions of the famous scientist. Now and then a magazine or newspaper would print an article about him, and it was always difficult to believe that one man could have accomplished so much.

The tent flap opened and Professor Waldo emerged again. Harry saw that he had fixed peculiar round black things to his front and back paws. He carefully adjusted them, moving the straps that held them this way and that, and then he placed the one attached to his left front paw on the hull of the *Jo-Anne-Mae*. It made a soft, sighing noise and appeared to stick quite firmly as the Professor pulled himself up. It didn't budge. He applied the black thing tied to his right front paw to a spot a little higher, and pulled himself up again.

"I've never seen anything quite like that, Harry," said Fred.

Now the Professor attached to the boat the black things fixed to his rear paws. He released the first one, which came loose with a gentle plopping. He paused, and then reapplied it a little higher up.

"You are seeing the Professor employing his latest invention, lads," said the Commodore. "It is his suction climber, and with it he can mount any given surface at any given angle."

"Why, it's wonderful!" said Harry, watching the Professor steadily coming closer. "We could certainly use something like that in the spy business!"

"I am sure the Professor would be happy to let you do so, but he has told me he does not wish to release it to the general public as he is afraid it would take all the fun out of mountain climbing."

Fred looked thoughtfully down at the Professor, who was now almost level with the deck.

"Gee, I don't know," he said. "It kind of looks like fun to me."

"Hello, Commodore," said the scientist, now coming easily over the railing. "How are you today?"

*The first one came loose with
a gentle plopping.*

"Shipshape, sir," answered the Navy bear. "And happy
to tell you these two fine bears by my side are the spies we
asked for."

"Ah," said the Professor, and after carefully removing

the suction climber from his paws, he gave a firm paw-shake to Harry and Fred. "I am glad you have come to help us with our sea serpent problem, and I think I may have just come across some information which will be useful to us."

"That's good news, sir," said the Commodore.

"I think it is, I think it is," said the Professor. "I believe I know where the monster has his lair!"

"Well, that is fine!" said the Commodore.

Harry smiled and nodded, but deep down inside he felt things were moving a little too fast.

"Yes," said the Professor. "From my calculations of the angle of vision of all reported sightings, including a rather dramatic new one of mine which I will tell you about, plus my analysis of recent weed disturbance, and to certain negative evidence, and the application of a theorem I don't see any sense in going into now, I have come to the conclusion that the sea serpent probably lives somewhere about Left Bear Paw Island."

"Oh, dear," said the Commodore.

"What do you mean?" asked Harry.

"Well, it's just that Left Bear Paw Island is a very unpleasant place, that's all. Probably the most unpleasant

"I am glad you have come to help us."

place within, oh, say seventy-five to a hundred miles any way from Beartown-on-the-Sea. Wouldn't you go along with that, Professor?"

"Oh, yes," said the scientist. "It's a miserable place. Horrible climate, depressing rock formations, all sorts of nasty, crawly things living there."

"Not to mention Little George and Big George. Just having them around a place would make it unpleasant enough all by itself," said the Commodore.

"Who are Big George and Little George?" asked Harry.

"They run the lighthouse at Lighthouse Point on Left Bear Paw Island," said the Commodore, "and they are probably the crankiest bears in all of Bearmania. I suggest you avoid them if at all possible, since being around them tends to get very unpleasant. They are brothers and I am glad I never met any of the rest of their family."

"I never heard of two brothers named George," said Fred.

"It may be what has made them so cranky," said Professor Waldo.

"In any case," said the Commodore, "all things considered, Left Bear Paw Island is not the sort of place I fancy poking around. Least of all for a sea serpent."

"Where is this Left Bear Paw Island?" asked Harry.

"You see that thing out there?" asked the Commodore, pointing.

Harry looked and saw a grim, craggy bulk out a half mile or so, with greenish mist around its edges. He had noticed it while he had been on vacation, walking around in his orange and yellow suit, and thought it was a shame to have such an unpleasant-looking thing in a place which was otherwise so bright and cheerful, and he wondered at the time why somebody didn't do something about it. Cart it away or something.

"Now do you understand?" asked the Commodore.

Harry was afraid he did.

Left Bear Paw Island

five Green Blurs

After the two spies had studied the bleak shape of Left
Bear Paw Island through the Commodore's copper telescope, they became pretty depressed at the thought of going there and hunting a sea serpent, but suddenly the
Commodore pulled a big brass watch out of his pocket
and said something which quickly cheered them up:

"It's lunchtime, mates. What say we tack over to the
Sailor's Rest and have ourselves a nice bowl of chowder?"

They went to the nice building with the flower-boxes,
from which they had previously smelled such delicious
smells, and settled themselves in the cozy dining room.
The Commodore called it a "mess," which was the authen-
tic naval term, but it seemed to Harry to be all very
scrubbed-looking and neat. The Commodore, sitting at the
head of the table, cleared his throat and looked over at
Sailor Ned, who was standing by the kitchen door.

"Ready, Ned?" asked the old salt.

"Ready, sir," replied Ned.

*"Where e'er you sail,
Bearmania."*

And then the two seamen broke into the following
song:

"Where e'er you sail,

Bearmania,

We'll sail along with you;

We'll never fail

Bearmania,

Ne'er wail upon the blue!"

The Commodore cleared his throat again and looked
apologetically at his guests.

"I hope you don't mind, mates," he said, "but it is our

time-honored custom to sing the Bearmanian National Sea Chanty before partaking of our meals."

"Not at all, sir," said Harry, who had, in fact, found the little ceremony very touching.

Sailor Ned turned out to be the cook of the Navy base, and a very good cook he was. He staggered into the mess carrying a bowl of fish chowder almost as big as himself, and then came back with biscuits and butter, and sat down with the rest of them and they all ate together. The Bearmanian Navy was a very relaxed, friendly sort of organization which did not believe in the separation of officers and enlisted men as did the sea forces of many other nations.

"My," said Harry, "this is one of the best soups I have ever had!"

Sailor Ned beamed and at once spooned another steaming portion into the fat bear's plate.

"You've pleased Ned mightily by calling his chowder 'soup,' lad," said the Commodore, "as he has a strong distaste for nautical terms or any kind of seafaring slang."

"Bunch of silly twaddle," observed Sailor Ned.

"Oh," said Harry, suddenly remembering. "Then I am sorry for the way I addressed you this morning."

"Don't worry about it for a minute," said Ned, smiling at Harry. "I understand you were only trying to be polite."

"Outside of that one little quirk," said the Commodore, "Ned, here, is as salty a sailor who ever trod a deck."

"As you, sir," said Ned, "are the best officer who ever set a course."

"Why, that's fine of you to say, Ned," said the Navy bear, "but there *is* my one failing of command."

"Why that's nothing, sir. It's of no importance at all."

The Commodore sighed and looked at Harry.

"I don't suppose you noticed anything odd about the *Jo-Anne-Mae,* did you, lad?" he asked the spy.

Harry thought a moment.

"It struck me as being one of the prettiest boats I've ever seen," said Harry.

"Did it now?" asked the old salt, brightening.

Professor Waldo, who had up until now been absorbed in making complicated-looking notes, looked up and said, "My goodness, Commodore, haven't I ever said how beautiful I think the *Jo-Anne-Mae* is?"

"Why no, Professor," said the Commodore, bewildered and pleased all at the same time, "you never did."

"Allow me to say it now, then. I think it is the loveliest ship afloat."

"You see, sir," said Sailor Ned gently, "I told you it was nothing to worry about."

Then the story came out and Harry and Fred and Professor Waldo learned that the Commodore had for some years now been unable to make up his mind which color to paint the *Jo-Anne-Mae,* and that was why Ned had painted one part this color and the other part that color, except for the gold trim and the lettering, which the Commodore had decided on right off.

"Being unable to make a decision is a very awkward thing for a naval officer," said the old salt. "But now you all say you think the *Jo-Anne-Mae* is nice with all those different hues. And you know I believe that I do, too. I have liked her all along, which may have been what confused me."

He sat up straight in his chair and turned to Ned.

"I believe I have come to a command decision!" he said.

"Sir!" said Sailor Ned, coming to his feet and saluting.

"I command that the *Jo-Anne-Mae* be left just as she is this very minute, unless either one of us thinks of some new color which might be nice to put here or there!"

"Aye aye, sir!" said Sailor Ned, and Harry was very touched that the small bear had thoughtfully employed one of the nautical terms he so disliked in order to make his reply sound as official as possible.

After this happy development, the bears cleaned up their lunch dishes and retired to the front room where

"I believe I have come to a command decision!"

they all settled down to talk about their plans concerning the sea serpent.

"It was a close call," said the Professor, who had taken charge of the discussion. "Perhaps, too close. For I think it almost got me."

"Er," said Fred. "Got you?"

"Yes," said the Professor, and he pulled out his wallet and extracted some photos which he passed around.

"Belay me," exclaimed the Commodore excitedly, "I've never seen this lot before, Professor!"

"I just took these pictures last week," said the scientist. "I am sorry they are all rather out of focus, but I was nervous at the time and unable to give the camera full attention. It's another invention of mine which works along somewhat different lines than an ordinary camera as the lens is flexible and is supposed to adjust to light as a living eye would; only I'm afraid I haven't quite got it flexible enough."

The pictures certainly were out of focus. Everything was blurred and fuzzy, but Harry privately thought that it was just as well, for had they been any clearer he would really have been depressed.

The first photo showed a far-off green blur which wasn't much of anything.

"At that point," explained the scientist, "I wasn't at all sure what I was seeing."

The second photo showed the green thing larger and lumpy-looking, with a hint of orange on its upper sides.

"By now I realized what it was and that I had attracted its attention, as it had begun to swim purposefully in my direction."

The third photo showed a big green thing with large round orange spots on either side, and a lot of smaller green things trailing along behind it.

"When I took this photo the serpent was only several yards from me—the orange spots are its eyes, by the way—and, in spite of rowing as hard as I could, I wasn't able to pull away from it. This experience was what convinced me to install a powerful motor in the floating tent."

The fourth and last photo in the series had a kind of green blur all around the edge and a lot of long white things poking this way and that toward its center.

"This is a picture of the interior of the serpent's mouth," said the Professor, clearing his throat. "And those white things are some of its teeth. I shot this photo

Had they been any clearer Harry really would have been depressed.

just before I climbed up the side of the cliff, which I had fortunately reached."

Harry looked at the picture and felt prickly all over, but he was careful to appear unworried.

"That was pretty close there, wasn't it?" said Fred, who did look worried.

"Yes, it was," admitted the Professor.

After a thoughtful pause, particularly thoughtful on the part of Harry and Fred, the bears began to plan.

Of course it was obvious the next step was to investigate the island. Harry suggested that he and Fred and the Professor take the floating tent to look over the place while Ned and the Commodore worked at freeing the *Jo-Anne-Mae* from its bed of sea tulips.

"The only problem," said the Professor, "is that I think the floating tent could only support the combined weight of Fred and myself. But it is obvious Harry must come along on the expedition."

"Maybe you could tow me behind," said Harry, and instantly wished he had kept his mouth shut.

"That's an excellent idea," said the Professor, nodding.

"It will only take me an hour or so to build a simple raft with a green cover which we can fix to the floating tent with a rope."

"That's very clever of you, Harry," said Fred.

"Thank you," mumbled Harry.

"And very brave, too," said the Commodore. "When I think what the rapids around Left Bear Paw Island will do to a simple raft, it just makes me queasy!"

"Thank you," mumbled Harry again.

"Allow me to wish you the best of luck, sir," said Sailor Ned. "For if the tow rope breaks when you approach the island and encounter the rapids, you might find yourself spinning off onto the rocks which rim the island. And if that happens, your raft could easily break up and a bit of luck would come in very handy indeed, sir."

"Thank you," mumbled Harry, for the third and last time.

six A Rough Voyage

It was decided that the expedition to Left Bear Paw Island would take place that very afternoon, and that Harry and Fred and the Professor would spend the night on the island since, except for the Professor's close call, the sea serpent had almost always been seen in the moonlight.

Harry and Fred went back to their hotel to get some things for the trip and Harry, bearing in mind the rather alarming things the Commodore and Ned had said about the coastal area of the island, put his bright yellow and orange swimming suit on underneath his official spy clothes.

On the way back Harry stopped off at a quaint little shop and got some macaroons in a waterproof tin and some saltwater taffy in a paper bag. He figured it wouldn't hurt saltwater taffy any if sea water got on it, and might even perk it up a little.

By the time the two spies returned to the Navy base, Professor Waldo had finished the raft, green covering and

all. Harry walked around it thoughtfully, poking it gently now and then with his foot. It *seemed* alright, and he
was sure that Professor Waldo had done his very best with
it. But it did look smallish for a fat bear such as himself.

The Professor went down the side of the hull, using his
amazing suction climber, and attached the raft to the
floating tent. Then he signaled and the Commodore and
Ned lowered Harry and Fred to the water, using the
plank the small sailor employed when painting. Fred got
into the tent with the Professor, and Harry, after the
tiniest hestitation, got onto—"into" seemed too generous
a term—the raft and, following the Professor's instructions, pulled the green cover, which was made of canvas,
over him so that he looked like a floating green lump bobbing in the water.

The path the Professor had cut through the sea tulips
only a few hours earlier had almost grown completely
closed again, and it took the scientist quite a while to cut
his way back through the vegetation. But at last they
were in open water, and away they moved from the *Jo-
Anne-Mae,* as Ned and the Commodore settled themselves
to the task of clearing it of sea tulips.

The cover of the raft had a peephole and Harry peered

Harry stopped off at a quaint little shop.

through it as the tent pulled him along. The tent moved by means of a hand-operated squirting device which was mounted underneath it. The squirting device shot out powerful jets of water that pushed the tent along in a series of spurts, and not very even spurts at that. As he jerked and bobbled along, Harry thought, and not for the first time, that he should have been a tap dancer, or a cook, or something nice like that instead of a spy.

Left Bear Paw Island grew closer and closer, and the nearer they got to it, and the more that could be seen of it, the less Harry liked it. Perhaps, he told himself, it would look better if he weren't seeing it through a peep-hole while sitting on a raft which was bobbing up and

Left Bear Paw Island grew closer and closer.

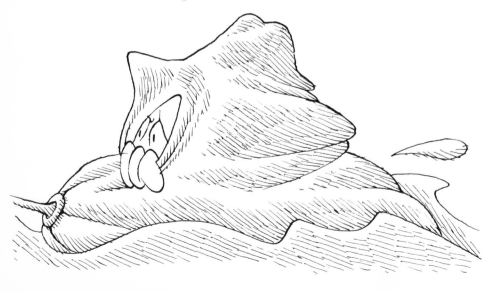

down and, at the same time, going ahead in an uneven series of jerks. But he didn't really think so.

From here he could see there was some vegetation on the thing; mostly scrawny trees with their branches all twisted and bent, nasty little bushes which Harry just knew had lots of thorns, and big patches of green mold which looked like the sort of stuff that showed up on potatoes if you left them in a damp place too long.

On the highest point of the island, which stuck up like a shark's fin, Harry could see the lighthouse which was tended by Big George and Little George. He had meant to ask more about them, but what he had already heard had been so unpleasant he had decided he would let the rest come as a surprise. He hoped the brothers wouldn't find out about their visit to the island, or, if they did, that they wouldn't do anything nasty.

Harry sighed and took the wax wrapping from a piece of saltwater taffy and put it in his mouth. It was very nice and chewy and tasted of peppermint, although it was colored blue. Harry had often wondered why they colored saltwater taffy in the odd colors they did. Then the raft began to do something which took Harry's mind right off saltwater taffy. It began moving in a very un-

comfortable zig-zag with a lot of bumps and many sur-
prising little lurches. Harry peered through his peephole,
rapidly chewing his taffy, and looked at the floating tent
up ahead.

What he saw wasn't reassuring. The rear flap of the
tent was open and Fred was halfway out, reaching up and
doing something to the cords that held the tent's top together. Fred was obviously following some instructions
from Professor Waldo, but he acted as if he wasn't sure
he had got them right or that he was accomplishing much
by carrying them out. He was clearly a worried bear and,
with the spray the waves were kicking up, an increasingly
wet one.

Harry sat back and worried a little, too, then he put his
eye to the peephole again only to see that things had obviously gotten worse. Now the top of the tent seemed to
have come partially undone, and, much worse, it had begun to spin this way and that, apparently unable to con-
trol its speed or direction. Fred was trying to tie some
ropes together and that was bad because Harry knew Fred
was just awful when it came to tying good knots. He just
never seemed to get the hang of it.

Sure enough, even as Harry watched, several knots

Things had obviously gotten worse.

which Fred must have tied while he wasn't looking came undone and half the roof of the tent flapped open and began beating in the air like a big green wing. Harry could see the Professor now, bent over something and working at it frantically.

By now the tent, with the raft swinging behind it, was going round and round in ever-widening circles. And Harry, hanging on for dear life, saw that the outside of the circle, which was where he was, was getting closer and closer to some sharp black rocks which were occasionally visible in the boiling surf.

Harry closed his eyes. There seemed to be absolutely no point in watching all this. He tried to think calm thoughts. He had read in a book somewhere that it was a good idea to think calm thoughts, and he had almost got hold of something calm to think about when he heard a loud, twanging noise. He looked out of the peephole and saw the green tent floating further and further away from him, tossing from one wave to the next. The rope which had held them together had snapped!

There was a sudden lurch and Harry pulled back from the peephole. For some reason, it had taken to squirting water like a trick flower he had bought years before in a novelty shop. Harry frowned at the squirting peephole, trying to understand why it was behaving in this fashion, but he found it hard to concentrate because of a peculiar sensation in his head. He reached up and found his hat was squashed between his head and the top of the covering of the raft. He had turned completely upside down!

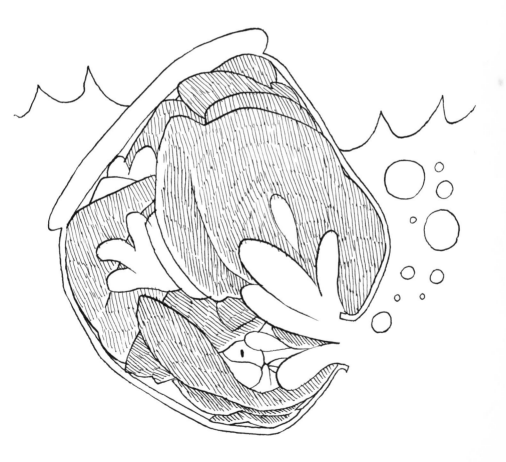

seven Left Bear Paw Island

When he thought about it later, Harry was never able to figure just how he got out of the raft. Perhaps the raft fell apart around him, perhaps he pulled it apart, perhaps it was torn apart by the sharp, black rocks; Harry would never know.

But he was always able to recall very clearly just how he felt once he was out from under the raft—and that was cold and wet and scared.

First the waves threw him way up high, and then they sucked him way down deep, and between the two he kicked his arms and legs and sometimes there would be water to kick against, and sometimes there would only be air, which was extremely disconcerting.

Harry looked around as well as he could and saw that he was being slowly driven closer to the stern, gray shore of Left Bear Paw Island, which was much better than being driven out to sea, but it was also dawning on him

64

that every time the waves sucked him down, they were taking him deeper and deeper.

Then he remembered from somewhere or other that wet clothes are heavier than dry clothes, and since his clothes were unmistakably and resoundingly wet, and since there was no way to dry them while bouncing around here in these waves, it would be a sensible thing to start taking them off.

He had only to remove his big official spy cloak to see he was on the right track, for it made him feel pounds lighter, and the next time the waves sucked him down they did not take him near so deep; so he continued to strip himself, piece by piece, until he was left only with his official spy hat and his bright orange and yellow striped bathing suit, and, of course, the tin of macaroons. Frankly, he felt a lot better.

Right around this time several waves got together and gave Harry a terrific shove and the next thing he knew he had been tossed against a big black rock. He clung there for a moment, trying to get his breath back, and then began to inch his way up the rock. In time he reached a point where the rock leveled off with a hollowed-out place that fit Harry's round body perfectly.

Several waves got together.

"That's more like it," said Harry to himself, feeling a bit snug and almost cozy on the rock. "Yes, sir, that's more like it," and then, exhausted, he closed his eyes, sighed, and was instantly sound asleep.

When Harry woke up he was a bit surprised at where he found himself. He raised up and looked around. The surf seemed to have quieted down some, and he could tell from the position of the sun that quite a bit of time had gone by. He got to his feet and, holding a paw over his eyes to shade them, he looked out to sea, but could see no sign of the floating green tent.

"I'm sure that Fred and the Professor are alright," he said to himself, and swallowed, for he was really not all that sure. "They'll get ashore safe and sound."

Now Harry set himself to getting a little further from the sea which had given him such a buffeting. He climbed from the big rock to a bigger one next to it and from it to a bigger one still and at last he was on the island itself, which was really not much more, it seemed to him, than the biggest rock of them all.

He opened the waterproof tin, found that it had worked, and ate a nice, dry macaroon, which made him feel a lot better and a lot more optimistic all around. He started to walk along the stony ground, avoiding the bushes which were thorny, and tried to figure what to do next. They had a slogan at the Bearmanian Spy Academy which went: "A Good Spy Is a Well-Organized Spy."

The first thing to do was to figure out where he was on Left Bear Paw Island. He looked around for a familiar landmark and saw one right off. There, right spang in front of him, was the lighthouse which was run by Big and Little George, but seeing it didn't make him exactly happy.

Slowly, not wanting to appear to be in a rush about it, Harry turned around and began to walk away from the lighthouse. All he had to do was make it back behind the rock and he wouldn't see the lighthouse again.

"Hey, you!" said a big, gruff voice behind him.

Harry paused.

"You!" said the voice again.

Harry turned, carefully, wearing what he hoped was a friendly little smile.

"Yes?" he said, and then his mouth went dry for there before him was the biggest bear he had ever seen. It has to be Big George, figured Harry, because if he's Little George and Big George is bigger than he is, I don't even want to think about how big Big George is.

"Who are you?" asked the enormous bear.

"Harry," said Harry. "How do you do? Are you Big George?"

It had to be Big George.

The enormous bear looked at Harry suspiciously.

"I'm Big George alright, but how come you know my name?" he asked.

Relieved that this was, after all, the biggest George, Harry looked at him carefully.

His entire outfit was bright yellow from his sou'wester to his rainslicker to his huge boots. He had little, beady eyes and great big teeth, and his hair grew out in spikes. Harry decided it would be a swell idea not to get Big George mad.

"Commodore Horatio told me your name, Big George," he said.

Big George frowned and had just opened his mouth to answer when a voice from the top of the lighthouse shrieked: "Shut up!"

Big George closed his mouth obediently and looked up, as did Harry, and there, standing on the little walkway which ran all around the top of the lighthouse, was perhaps the smallest bear Harry had ever seen. He glared down furiously at them both.

"I've told you not to talk to strangers," said the little bear, who was also dressed in a bright yellow rainproof outfit, and could be none other than Little George. "Now, haven't I? Haven't I? Haven't I told you not to talk to strangers?"

The huge bear blinked.

"Yes, Little George," he said.

"Well, then," said the little bear, *"don't talk to strangers!"*

"Shut up!"

Then the little bear vanished into the lighthouse and Harry could hear his tiny feet clinking down the metal steps inside the building. In no time at all, Little George shot out of the lighthouse door and scuttled over to squint up angrily at the fat bear spy.

"*I'm* the one who talks to strangers," said Little George, still shouting even though he was now right next to Harry. "*And they usually wish I hadn't!*"

eight A Run Along the Water

Although they did not have an easy time of it, Fred and Professor Waldo's landing on the island was not nearly as dramatic as Harry's. The Professor had finally managed to get his water motor going again, Fred had gotten all the knots tied right at last, and, after surviving a very scary ride among the sharp, black rocks, they found a rocky cove in which to come ashore.

"I do hope Harry is alright," said Fred, helping the scientist to tie down the green tent so that it would not be carried out by the tide. "That last glimpse I got of him looked pretty grim!"

"He is an intelligent and resourceful bear, and I have every confidence he will make his way safely," said the Professor. "But we shall look for him before doing anything else just in case he does need help."

After they were sure the tent was snug, the two bears left the cove and set off to find Harry. They walked along the coast, the Professor looking inland and Fred gazing

It was rugged climbing at times.

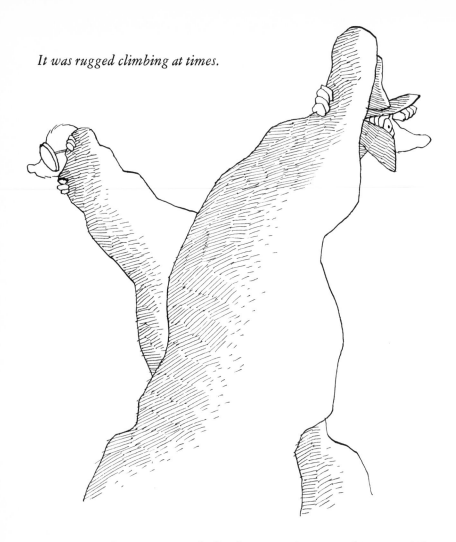

out to sea. It was rugged climbing at times, and it was difficult to make sure they had seen everything, as big, view-
blocking rocks were everywhere.

They had been walking for about a half an hour when

Fred took hold of the Professor's arm and pointed out to sea.

"Oh, my gosh—look!" cried Fred.

There, bobbing on the surf, between some particularly sharp-looking rocks was a large, round, black shape.

The two bears wasted no time in scrambling down to see what it was for they were dreadfully afraid it might be Harry, but it was only his official spy cape.

"What do you think this means, Professor?" asked Fred.

"Well," began the scientist, and there was no doubt his voice had a pretty gloomy sound to it, but then he stopped and began again. "Look, Fred, ahead—what do you see?"

It was another patch of black bobbing about, and this time it was easy to tell from a distance, on account of its size and shape, that it was Harry's pants.

"And look over there," said the Professor, pointing further ahead at what was surely Harry's coat.

"And look, Professor, oh, look way over there on that rock!" cried Fred very happily, for there, far away but in clear view, sound asleep in his bright orange and yellow bathing suit, was none other than Harry himself!

"Excellent!" said the Professor. "Now all we have to do is get to him!"

That did not prove to be at all simple, for climbing to the rock where Harry lay dozing meant that they had to climb up and down a good many rocks in between. Sometimes he was in their line of vision, sometimes not.

The last ten minutes or so of their climbing were the worst and Harry was completely out of their sight for the whole time.

"I believe we're almost there," said the Professor.

"I think you're right, sir," said Fred.

But when the two bears pulled themselves up so that they were indeed looking at the very spot where Harry had been napping so peacefully for the last hour or so they found only a large damp spot where the fat bear had been!

"Darn!" said Fred, and the scientist had to agree.

"At least we know he's alright," said Professor Waldo.

Then they heard a screeching shout coming from above: "Get him! Get him! Get that fat bear!"

They heard a thumping and a puffing, and suddenly rounding a rock into their view, running as fast as he could, was Harry.

"What's happening, Harry?" asked Fred.

But Harry could only puff and point behind him as he ran around another rock and out of sight.

"What's happening, Harry?"

"What do you think that's all about?" asked Fred.

The scientist was frowning thoughtfully down at his feet.

"I've just noticed a very peculiar phenomenon," he said. "The ground is shaking beneath us."

Fred looked down and then nodded.

"You're right," he said. "Sort of in beats, as if someone were hitting it with something very heavy."

"I think you would get the same effect," said Professor Waldo, "if an elephant was running this way."

"Yes," said Fred. "Or something else very large."

Then, at the same time, the two bears got a glimpse of a huge mass of yellow bobbing toward them.

"Perhaps we should join Harry, Fred," said the scientist.

"I think that would be a swell idea, sir," said the thin bear spy.

The two began to run in the same direction Harry had taken and it wasn't too long before they saw their friend hurrying along ahead of them down a trail descending to the sea. They continued to follow him, gaining gradually as they did so.

"He appears to be slowing down a little," said the Professor.

"Harry never was much of a one for exercise," said Fred.

The trail now ran alongside the sea, with a sheer gray

cliff rising on its other side. The water sloshed over the path occasionally and the bears' feet splashed in it as they ran. By now the three bears were running together as a group, the Professor and Fred having caught up to Harry.

"Are you alright, Harry?" asked Fred.

"Nothing a little rest won't cure, Fred," gasped Harry.

"Certainly glad you didn't get hurt landing back there, Harry," said Fred.

"Thank you, Fred," said Harry.

Then the path widened and the bears found themselves running past a grotto, a kind of cave with rock formations which had been weathered over the years by surf and wind into strange shapes that looked like hunching goblins and crawling lizards and other weird creatures.

"Wait a second," said the Professor. "I think I have an idea."

They slowed to a halt, and then, with the scientist taking the lead, they worked their way back into the grotto. Harry momentarily mistook one twisty-looking rock for a giant octopus, and that gave him a bit of a turn, but he didn't let on.

"We can hide ourselves here," said the Professor, "and let Big George, for I assume that large yellow object I made out through the trees back there was Big George—"

"It was," said Harry.

"—we'll just let Big George run right on past us and go on running for as long as he likes."

It seemed an excellent idea to Harry for, truth be told, although he was a very brave bear and willing to do absolutely anything which must be done in the name of a safer Bearmania, he wasn't sure if he could have run too much further.

So they settled themselves deep in the grotto, hidden behind a big rock which looked like it had horns and claws. Soon the earth began to shake beneath them again, and shortly after that the enormous bulk of Big George in his yellow outfit thumped past the entrance to the cave.

They sat very still until the ground-shaking subsided, and then they sat still some more, just to be on the safe side. Harry opened his tin of macaroons, and passed it around, and each bear had a little snack, and Harry told them of his adventures.

"Little George kept yelling and carrying on something fierce," Harry said, coming to the end of his story. "And he started to tell Big George to do something to me, but by then it was difficult to make out what he was saying,

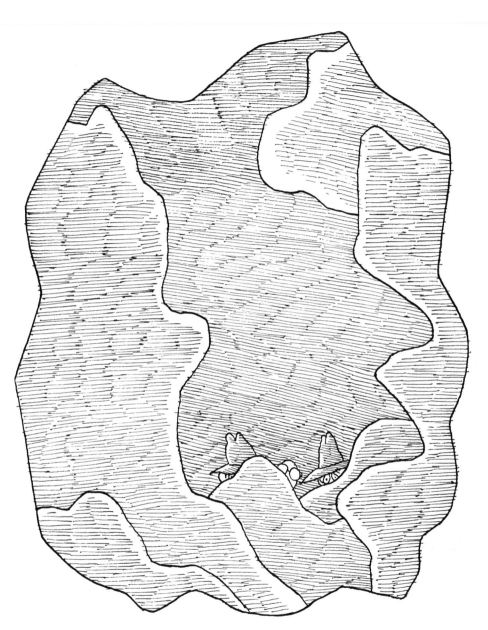

"We can hide ourselves here."

he was screeching so. I don't really know what it was he had in mind, but I *did* know *whatever* it was, Big George would do it. So I figured the best thing to do was leave."

"I think you were right, Harry," said Fred.

"Yes, I believe that was the intelligent move," said Professor Waldo.

"Well, you certainly didn't exaggerate one little bit about those Georges," said Harry, removing his hat and wiping his brow. "Are they always that cranky?"

"Always," said the scientist.

nine A Surprise Visitor

By now the shadows had grown very long and the bears had grown very tired and so, after a brief discussion, everybody decided it would be a good idea to take a little nap in order to be fresh and ready for some serious sea-serpent-watching that night. They found themselves a snug spot, set well back from the grotto's entrance, had one more macaroon apiece, and then went right off to sleep—which is something that comes easily to bears.

Sometime later Harry found himself awakened, but not quite sure what had done it. Following spy training for such occasions, he did not sit up, but kept in the same position, pretending he was still asleep. He opened his eyes just the tinest bit and looked this way and that without moving his head and, right in front of him, he saw something white and shaggy!

It took a lot of will power not to open his eyes wide, but Harry managed it. He watched the white shaggy thing carefully, still breathing deeply and regularly as a bear does when he's sleeping, and then he saw the white thing slowly reach out toward the macaroon tin he held in his paws and suddenly it came to him—he had been awakened by a tugging feeling on his macaroon box!

Slowly, stealthily, the white thing's paw took hold of the box and began to tug at it gently, and Harry wondered what he should do next. He decided the time for action had come, so, without any warning, and with remarkable agility and quickness for a bear of his fatness, Harry sprang up and grabbed the white box tugger!

It squealed and squeaked and carried on, waking the Professor and Fred, but though it struggled and writhed about very cleverly, it never got free of Harry's firm grip. The Professor took a sulphur match from a waterproof pocket in his shirt, lit it, and held it high, and for the first time Harry's catch was clearly visible.

"My gosh," said Fred. "It's a little, old, wrinkled bear!"

"Who are you?" asked Harry.

"I forget who!" said the white old bear.

"What do you mean, you forget who," said Fred, disgustedly. "That's silly!"

"You try living all by yourself for years and years and

A white shaggy paw took hold of the box!

years and see how much you remember!" said the old bear.

"How many years?" asked Harry.

"I forget," said his small captive. "That's what I came here all those years and years ago to do—to forget! And it worked! I don't remember a thing!"

And here the old bear cackled wildly, quite pleased and proud of himself.

"I know who that is, now," cried the Professor. "That's

the Hermit of Left Bear Paw Island! He's only been seen a very few times through the years as he's very good at hiding."

"Who was he before he became a hermit?" asked Harry.

"Nobody knows," said the Professor.

"Nobody knows!" echoed the Hermit, gleefully. "Not even me! Isn't it wonderful?"

"I think he's a little dotty," muttered Fred.

"No, sir, I was dotty to be who I was before, whoever that was, because it was terrible being him. That much I remember—it was just awful!" cried the shaggy white bear.

The Hermit brooded over what he had said a moment, and broke into laughter.

"But I'm not him, anymore, whoever he was—I'm me, whoever me is!"

"Do you think this is getting us anywhere, Harry?" asked Fred.

Harry studied the peculiar bear for a long moment.

"I'll bet he could tell us about the sea serpent," said Harry.

"I think you're right," said the Professor. "He knows this island if anyone does."

"I bet I could," cackled the Hermit, "but I bet I don't!"

"Why not?" asked Harry.

"Because hermits don't tell things. Everybody knows that!" said the wrinkled bear.

"Seems to me you've already done a lot of talking," said Fred.

"Yes," admitted the Hermit, "but I haven't made any sense!"

Harry thought, and then he turned to his fellow spy.

"Bring me the macaroon tin, Fred, please. It fell on the ground over there during the struggle."

Fred brought the box over. The Hermit pretended to ignore it, but he kept stealing eager looks at it out of the corners of his eyes.

"That's how he woke me up in the first place," said Harry. "Trying to borrow my macaroons. I believe he'd like one. Open the box, Fred."

Fred did so and the Hermit's eyes widened noticeably. In spite of an obvious effort not to do so, he licked his lips.

"Give the poor old fellow a macaroon, Fred," said Harry.

Grudingly, Fred took a macaroon from the box and held it out to the Hermit who, after a moment of pretended

"Hermits don't tell things, everybody knows that!"

indifference, grabbed it and popped it into his shaggy mouth.

"I thought so," said Harry.

"My goodness, look at him," said Fred, watching the Hermit who was chewing the macaroon blissfully with his eyes closed, making little happy moans. "I don't think I've ever seen a bear enjoy a macaroon so much in my entire life!"

"Can you imagine how it must have been, Fred," said Harry sadly, "being without one single macaroon for all those years and years?"

"Oh, that's an awful thought!" said Fred.

The Hermit swallowed the macaroon slowly, as if regretting it was already over, and opened his eyes.

"Did you like that?" asked Harry gently.

"Oh, yes!" said the Hermit.

"I'm glad," said Harry.

"I wouldn't give him another macaroon for awhile, yet," said the Professor. "After all this time without them it's hard to guess what a lot of macaroons at once might do to his system."

"Alright, then," said Harry, "we'll give you another one after a little bit."

Then he let go of the Hermit and stood back, looking carefully at the shaggy white bear to see if he would run, but he didn't.

"In a way I wish you hadn't done that," said the Hermit thoughtfully, sucking at a bit of macaroon on one of his teeth. "It makes me wonder if I've done the right thing for all these years. I'd forgotten macaroons, too, you see."

"And comfortable slippers," said Harry.

"That's right," said the Hermit, nodding, looking a little wistful.

"And railroad schedules," said Fred.

The Hermit glanced at him. "I never did much care for railroad schedules," said the Hermit. "As a matter of fact they're one of the reasons I'm here."

Fred, who was, as a matter of fact, very fond of railroad schedules, and forms, and charts, and efficient things like that, found the Hermit very difficult to understand.

"Well, anyway," said the Hermit, scratching the shaggy top of his head, "it's suddenly occurred to me there'd be no great harm done if I modified my ways."

He looked at Harry.

"I don't suppose you could manage to get me some slippers, could you?"

"I think that could be arranged," said Harry.

"Nice red ones, with a woolly lining?"

"I know a store in Beartown-on-the-Sea that has some just like that," said Professor Waldo. "I'll be happy to see that a pair gets to you."

"Well, that would be nice," said the Hermit, sighing contentedly. Then, after a pause, he said, "So you're interested in the sea serpent, are you?"

"Yes, we are," said Harry. "Can you tell us anything about it?"

"Oh, I can do more than that," said the shaggy little bear. "I can lead you to it!"

ten The Sighting

Harry and Fred and Professor Waldo followed the Hermit in the moonlight as he led them down paths winding through groves of twisted trees, and along narrow passes between towering boulders, and up and down trails slanting across the faces of rugged cliffs, and were amazed at the way the old bear leaped and capered ahead of them so tirelessly.

"You don't suppose," Fred whispered to Harry once as they were struggling up the side of a particularly steep incline while the Hermit sat high above waiting for them to catch up, "that he's playing some kind of joke on us?"

"I don't think so, Fred," said Harry. "Though he does have a peculiar sense of humor."

"And I'd just like to know what he's got against railroad schedules!" muttered Fred, pulling his cloak loose from a thorn bush.

Eventually it became obvious that although the Hermit might be an oddly whimsical sort of a bear, he was leading

"He does have a peculiar sense of humor."

the little expedition to a perfectly sensible destination for spotting sea serpents, because they ended up standing on a high plateau which commanded a sweeping view of the sea between Left Bear Paw Island and Wrecked Bear Reef, the very area where the monster had been most frequently spotted.

The Hermit, sprightly as ever, pranced over to the edge of the plateau and spread his shaggy white arms to indicate the view.

"If it takes it into its mind to have a swim tonight, here is where you'll see it!" he cackled.

"Have you seen it yourself?" asked Harry.

"Of course I have, but I keep out of sight, so it's never seen *me!* Same as the Georges over there," he said, pointing at the lighthouse which was in clear view but quite some distance away. "They haven't seen me yet, not one time!"

Harry sat down on a rock, for the climb had been pretty rugged, and studied the impressive seascape before him. Far out the foam was frothing along the length of Wrecked Bear Reef where many a brave bear ship had foundered and gone down, beyond that was a wide and wavy stretch of the Great Bear Sea, and, beating on the shore closer be-

low, was the spray and spume of the island's rugged surf.
All in all, Harry had to admit, it was quite some sight.

"Harry," said Professor Waldo, "would you look over
here, please? I'm not sure I'm seeing what I think I'm
seeing and could use a second opinion."

Harry joined the scientist and peered out with him in
the same direction.

"What do you think you see, sir?" he asked.

"I'd rather you spotted it for yourself, Harry, that is, if
it's happening at all."

Harry put his paws behind his back, pursed his lips, and
began to make a thoughtful catalogue of the view before
him.

"Well," he said, "there's the moon, of course. Which is
full. And round. There are a lot of rocks over there to the
left, and lots more over to the right, and quite a bit more
in the middle. Let's see, now, then there are some thorn
bushes growing right here in front with—I'd never noticed
them before—with little white flowers. Pretty little things.
Then there's the lighthouse . . ."

Harry paused.

". . . which is putting out a green light," he finished.

"So I didn't imagine it," said Professor Waldo.

"I'm not sure I'm seeing what I think I'm seeing."

"No, sir," said Harry, "that's a green light it's putting out, there, no doubt about it."

Harry turned.

"Fred," he said, "would you come over here for a moment and tell me if you notice anything unusual?"

"Glad to, Harry," said Fred, joining Harry and the scientist.

He looked out at the view before him.

"It's the lighthouse, Harry," he said without a moment's hesitation. "It's putting out a green light."

The Hermit had joined them and now he cackled and said, "That's not all—sometimes it shines bright red! But you've got more interesting stuff to look at than a lighthouse, and if you give me a macaroon, I'll tell you what it is!"

Harry looked at the Professor.

"Do you figure it's safe to give him another, sir?" he asked.

"I believe so, Harry," Professor Waldo answered. "He seems to have taken the first one in stride."

The Hermit chewed and swallowed the macaroon with as much pleasure as he had before, and then he looked up thoughtfully at the sky.

"Yes," he mused, "I really think I may have made a mistake, back then. Was it really all that bad being me, whoever I was? Was it worth giving up all those macaroons?"

"Come on, now," said Fred, who was a stickler for promises. "What was it you were going to show us?"

"Oh, that," said the Hermit. "Certainly."

He turned to face the sea and pointed with one of his shaggy, white arms.

"Look to the far left end of Wrecked Bear Reef and you'll see it, alright," he said.

Harry and Fred and Professor Waldo did as the Hermit told them to do and, as one bear, they gasped in astonishment.

"There it is!" cried Harry. "There's the sea serpent!"

"Oh, I wish I had my telescope," said Professor Waldo.

"My goodness, it really is awfully big, isn't it?" asked Fred in a voice which was slightly smaller than usual.

There, apparently swimming from beyond the surf that foamed about the base of Wrecked Bear Reef, it was, clearly lit by the moon, and looking very much like the drawing which Commodore Horatio had shown the two spies. Only, if anything, the real thing looked even worse as it seemed very, very long, so long that it appeared really to trail off in a peculiar fashion, making it difficult to say just where it ended, and the head was definitely much, much worse than the drawing!

"Er," said Fred, "I hadn't realized its eyes shone in the dark!"

"It's a detail new to me, too, Fred," said Professor Waldo. "Perhaps it's some trick of the moonlight."

"And its, ah, teeth," said Fred. "My gracious, they're so big you can see them clearly all the way from here."

"Yes," admitted Harry. "It certainly does have great big teeth!"

"How do you like it, hey?" asked the Hermit, quite pleased with the effect the sea serpent was producing. "You don't see a sight like that every day!"

"Look, Harry," said Professor Waldo. "It seems to be heading for the very cove where we beached the floating tent!"

"You're right, Professor, so it is," said Harry.

"I suppose we'd better go down and meet it and see what happens then," said Fred.

"That's the ticket, Fred!" said Harry.

eleven The Serpent Watchers

The climb down to the cove was a good deal easier than the climb up had been. Fred almost took one nasty tumble, but Harry grabbed him just in time. Everybody got scratched a little by thorns, but, by and large, it wasn't all that bad.

The first thing they did was to peer out into the Great Bear Sea to see if the sea serpent was still heading for the cove and, sure enough, they could see it, way out there, headed unmistakably for them. The second thing they did was to check out the floating tent to see if it was safe, which it was. And the third thing they did, under the Professor's careful instructions, was to take various pieces of equipment from the tent and put them in working order.

"I'm certainly glad to get my paws back on this," said the Professor, carefully setting up an ingenious-looking telescope.

He aimed the device and looked through it intently.

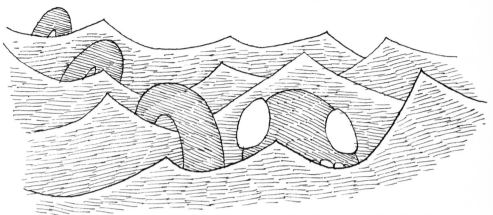

"Its eyes really do glow in the dark."

"Oh, it's even better than I'd hoped," said Professor Waldo. "Here, Harry, have a look."

Harry put his eye to the telescope and, giving the view-finder a turn or two to adjust to his particular focus, he saw the sea serpent as it would look if it were only a short distance away.

"Well," he said, "one thing is certain—its eyes really do glow in the dark."

"You're right, Harry," said Professor Waldo. "That's decidedly no trick of the moonlight."

"And you're right about its teeth, Fred," said Harry. "They really are enormous. Without a doubt the biggest teeth I've ever seen anywhere. Would you care to take a look?"

"That's alright, Harry," said Fred. "I figure I'll be seeing them soon enough."

"Could I take a peek?" asked the Hermit.

"Of course," said Harry, and he stood aside and showed the wrinkly old bear how to work the telescope.

"Why, this thing is wonderful," breathed the Hermit, moving the telescope this way and that. He turned it away from the sea and up and, after a moment of searching with it, gave a little cackle.

"Look here," he said. "Little George has got one, too!"

Harry and the Professor each looked in turn and saw that the Hermit had angled the telescope so that the top of the lighthouse was framed in its lens, and there was Little George, all lit up green from the green light that was shining from the lighthouse lamp, holding a telescope, peering through it intently, and gnashing his teeth absent-mindedly.

"It looks as if we're not the only bears watching sea serpents tonight," said Harry.

The Professor pulled a flat bag from the floating tent and began to undo the numerous straps which held it shut. He had an air of purpose about him which drew the other bears.

*Little George was peering
through the telescope.*

"What is that, sir?" asked Harry, as the scientist undid
the last strap and began to draw the bag open.

"It is, I think, the only sea serpent net ever constructed.
I believe that with it we will be able to capture the creature without harming it, and my dream is to study it and

perhaps train it to carry out useful jobs, rather as elephants do in India."

Harry looked admiringly at Professor Waldo, thinking how few bears would ever have thought of such a thing. Certainly he knew he couldn't have done it. Not in a million years.

The Professor continued to work on the net, and Harry turned the telescope back to the sea monster so as not to miss any action on its part. It was a strange sensation to watch the creature coming closer and closer. Harry saw that its head was covered with many small green scales, and that its shining eyes were orange and wobbled as it swam, and that it had a huge yellow tongue in its mouth which seemed to constantly curl and uncurl.

The Professor dragged the floating tent to the edge of the sea, all shipshape and ready to float.

"I think there's a good chance we may have to pursue the serpent in the water, Harry," he said. "So I have the tent prepared, and I'd like to have you put these on so that we can tow you behind."

Harry was handed what looked like two large green rubber leaves fixed to a harness. Nervously, he strapped the

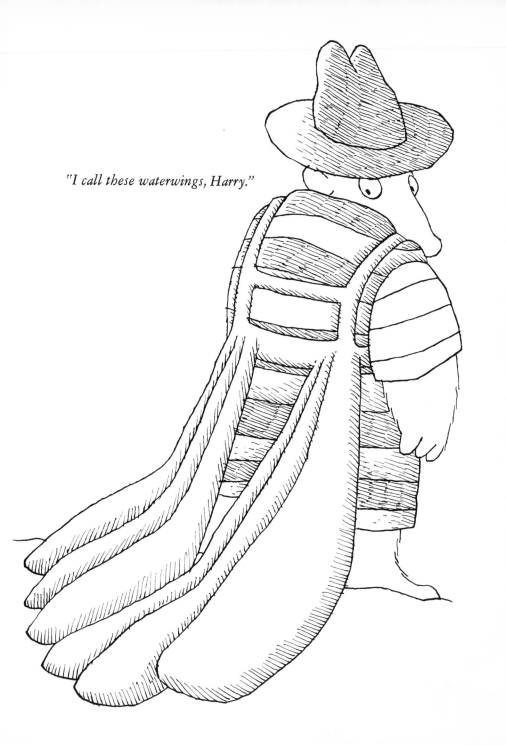

"I call these waterwings, Harry."

harness around his chest, the Professor helping, so that the leaves hung limply down his back.

"I call these waterwings, Harry," said the Professor. "If we take to the sea, merely pull this plug here"—he tapped a little red cork set into the harness just below Harry's chin—"and the wings will inflate. Just swim naturally and the wings will support you and flap with the forward motion, thus helping you along."

"Oh, Harry," called out Fred, who was sitting before the telescope on a folding stool the Professor had taken from the floating tent, "would you come here for a moment, please? And you, too, Professor?"

When they joined him, the thin bear stood and asked them to take a look at the serpent.

"I think it's changing course," said Fred.

"You're right," said the scientist. "I was afraid it was asking too much to have the creature swim right into our arms. It looks as if we will have to pursue it at sea. Fortunately we have readied ourselves for the occasion."

Harry and Fred helped the Professor push the floating tent into the water.

"I am afraid you will have to stay ashore," said Harry to the Hermit.

"That's alright," said the Hermit, eyeing the floating tent and Harry's waterwings. "I'd just as soon. Besides I'll be able to watch everything through the telescope."

So Fred and the Professor got into the tent and Harry, remembering only too clearly what had happened before, but taking account of the fact that the waves around Left Bear Paw Island seemed to quiet down a bit at night, was roped to the rear.

"Pull the red plug, Harry," said the Professor, and Harry did, and with a great whooshing sound, the wings filled with air and spread out behind him. At once Harry found himself comfortably supported in the water with no effort whatsoever.

"Alright, everybody," cried the Professor. "Here we go!" And with a smooth start of the water motor, and a wave good-bye from all to the Hermit, the three bears started off in pursuit of the sea serpent. Then Harry looked back and up and saw a puzzling thing.

"Fred and Professor Waldo," he called out. "Take a look at the lighthouse!"

They did and saw, as Harry had, that the light beaming from Lighthouse Point had turned from a murky green to a bright and flaming red!

twelve The Chase

The water was a good deal calmer than it had been before, Harry was grateful to note, and the waterwings made the towing experience not at all unpleasant, and actually sort of fun.

Whatever else the sea serpent was, it did not seem to be particularly fast, so the three bears did not have too much trouble keeping it well in sight.

It had changed course drastically from its heading to the cove, almost as if it had seen the bears waiting for it, and was now bearing for a craggy bit of the island's coast not too far ahead, getting closer and closer to land all the time.

It's up to something, thought Harry to himself. It's going to pull some sort of trick.

By now they seemed to be actually gaining on the monster and Harry began to wonder vaguely just what they would do when they caught up to it. The looping segments that made up its back glinted and glistened in the moonlight, and Harry found himself wondering just what the serpent would really look like on dry land. Would it be a long, sort of snaky thing, as in the Commodore's drawing, or would it perhaps be different? Even this close and getting closer it was very hard to figure out just exactly what it was he was seeing.

Suddenly Harry heard the Professor cry out: "Harry, look over there, toward the mainland!"

Harry did and had to gasp, for there, in full rigging with all her sails puffed full with wind, was the ship *Jo-Anne-Mae*. She looked beautiful in the moonlight, and moved in a proud and steady fashion. Commodore Horatio and Sailor Ned had got her free from her confining bed of sea tulips, and now she was well on her way to Left Bear Paw Island.

"Isn't she just lovely?" cried out Harry, and the three bears looked at her with admiration. She had been pretty enough moored to the pier at the Navy yard, but here on the high sea with the wind behind her and lit by the full moon, she was spectacular.

Harry turned to say something else to his companions, but whatever it was stopped in his mouth and was forgotten, because, looking beyond the floating tent to the shore of the island, Harry saw to his astonishment that the sea serpent was no longer in sight!

"It's gone!" he cried. "It's gone!"

Harry heard a confused muttering coming from the floating tent, and then Fred's head popped out.

"Did you see any sign of where it went, Harry?"

"No, Fred," the fat bear called out. "It's just gone!"

There was a rustling noise, and Harry saw that the top of the tent was being rolled down briskly by Professor Waldo, as Fred was tightening the screws on some new scientific device.

"I'm going to signal the ship, Harry," said the Professor, lighting a match and applying it to the wick of a lantern mounted on the top of the device. "And fill them in on what's happened so far."

Harry watched as the scientist flicked a clever shutter on and off the lantern lens, making the light appear to go off and on and by that means send a message in Naval Code to the approaching *Jo-Anne-Mae*. There was only the briefest pause after the Professor's message had ended before a flashing reply came speeding from the colorful vessel.

"I'm going to signal the ship, Harry."

"Search . . . the . . . coast," translated Professor Waldo aloud. "Look . . . for . . . cave."

Professor Waldo pointed the floating tent toward the

craggy coast without another word and they raced for it as Fred extinguished and folded up the signal machine. Harry, gliding along behind, carefully examined the steep cliffs as they neared them and eventually saw a twisting black fissure that looked like a lightning bolt carved out of the side of the gray stone, widening where it met the water into what could very well be the entrance to a cave.

"I think that's a cave," cried Harry. "At the end of that big crack in the cliff!"

Fred relayed Harry's message to the Professor, nodded back at his friend, and the floating tent aimed straight for the opening. In almost no time at all they were bobbing in the water before it.

"What do you think, Harry?" asked the Professor. "Should we go in?"

Harry frowned thoughtfully, making one of those difficult decisions that are part of a bear spy's life.

"You and Fred stay out here, for if the serpent runs you have the means to chase it," said Harry. "I will go in on the waterwings and see what I can see."

"Take along the net, Harry!" cried the Professor.

"I wouldn't know how to work it, sir," Harry called back.

"Oh, dear," murmured the scientist to himself. "All that work for nothing!"

Harry headed for the entrance, observing over his shoulder as he entered that the Professor was sending along

"I will go in on the waterwings," said Harry.

this latest bit of news to the *Jo-Anne-Mae* by means of the signal machine.

Inside the cave—for Harry had guessed right and this certainly was a cave—all was a brilliant blue as the moonlight shone through the cave opening and reflected on the water. The cave stretched back in a kind of curving tunnel, and Harry could not see beyond the curve. Without giving himself time to think about the advisability of the action, Harry swam forward.

Around the curve it began to get darker, but there was still plenty of light to see by, and Harry was frankly quite surprised by what he saw. He had expected any number of things, but never in his life, not if he had had hours and hours to try, would he have guessed that around the curve of the cave he would find himself swimming into a garden!

Of course he realized after a second what the pink and white flowers were, namely a huge bed of sea tulips, but it did not reduce the startling effect any. The cinnamon perfume of the tulips was very strong in the confines of the cave. Harry sniffed it and smiled and found it to be delicious. Then he heard a little ploshing sound in the water nearby and stiffened, for he had nearly forgotten he was looking for a monster.

As quietly as possible, he swam to one side of the cave where he found a handhold in the rock. Slowly, carefully, he edged up the uneven stone and was delighted to find a projection some four feet above the tulip garden big enough for him to sit on.

He sat absolutely still, hardly even breathing, the only noise he made being a slight dripping of water from his bathing suit and fur, and that soon stopped. Minutes passed and Harry continued to sit just as still as the rock on which he perched, silent as any bird-watcher waiting for a redbreasted grosbeak.

Then, as a reward for his patience, Harry heard once more the subtle ploshing noise.

He made no visible reaction at all, even though his heart sped up, and then came another plosh, and then another, and Harry began to see something or other moving amid the flowers of the water garden.

He looked around, being careful not to turn his head, and watched the movement grow and spread and then, one by one, he saw little heads popping up out of the water and realized a whole flock of strange little creatures had been floating concealed among the sea tulips.

As he watched, still as a statue, the creatures relaxed

and, before his eyes, began to feed happily on the tulips, eating them with gusto and much chomping, and occasionally playing with the flowers by tossing them into the air and catching them with their mouths. They made happy little woofing noises as they ate the flowers and played with them and Harry thought them perhaps the cutest beings he had ever seen, though he had no idea on earth what they were.

The creatures were about three feet long and had four flippers with tiny paws at the ends. Their heads seemed to join right onto their bodies without the benefit of a neck and were round as marbles. They had curious little eyes, which were forever looking this way and that, no nose in particular, and above their mouths they all had a sort of ridiculous green moustache which would often have a flower or two tangled in its strands. They were green except for their eyes, which were a lovely sort of honey color.

Suddenly, without any warning, the creatures all vanished with only three or four faint ploshes, and Harry found himself once again staring at what seemed to be a completely deserted garden. He gaped down at the flowers, wondering if he had imagined the little green creatures.

Then from a bend further back in the cave came an orange glow and, as he squeezed himself up into the smallest ball his fatness would allow, Harry watched the head of the sea serpent slowly round into sight.

It looked straight at him with its glowing orange eyes, and the fat bear could see its huge, yellow tongue working in its mouth as it slowly floated closer and closer until its nose bumped right into the rocky ledge, where Harry sat!

"WHAT ARE YOU DOING IN HERE?" boomed the sea serpent in a terrible echoey voice. *"YOU BAD, BAD BEAR!!!"*

That was one of the worst moments in his career as a professional spy, Harry was later to admit, but the absolutely most awful one came just a little later. He had pressed himself as hard as he could against the stone wall in order to get as far as he could from the horrible green head, with its big orange eyes wobbling and glowing and its hundreds of scales and dozens of teeth shining in the orange light, when he saw the huge yellow tongue of the thing uncoil and stretch out in order—or so Harry was absolutely certain at the time—to gulp him in and gobble him up!

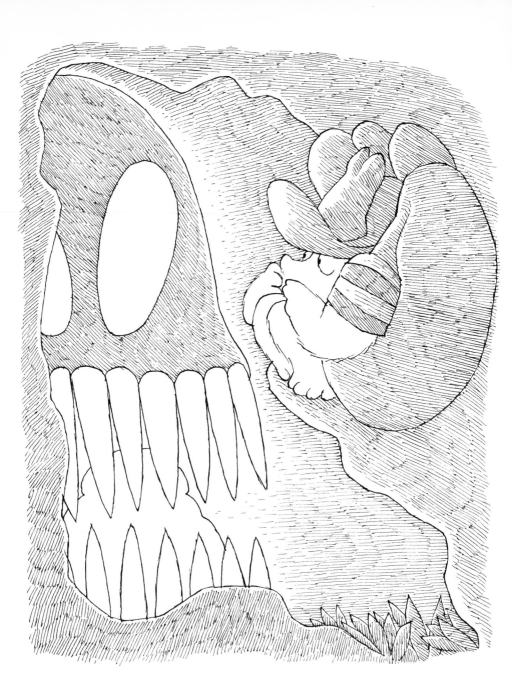

"WHAT ARE YOU DOING IN HERE?" boomed the sea serpent.

It is to the great credit of Harry and proof of his con-
siderable courage, though he never mentions it when he
tells the story, that he did not panic but instantly went
into action in order to try and protect himself.

Quickly, with a smooth movement, Harry pulled the
waterwings from his back and began to baff the nose of
the sea serpent with them as hard as he could, over and
over, and he saw to his astonishment that he had suc-
ceeded in banging the enormous left green nostril shut.

"STOP THAT!" cried the horrible, hollow voice of the
monster. *"YOU'LL BUST IT AND I'LL BE IN TROU-
BLE!"*

Harry paused, as even in this extreme situation it struck
him as a peculiar thing for a sea serpent to say.

"What do you mean?" he found himself asking.

*"IF YOU MESS UP THE HEAD, LITTLE GEORGE
WON'T LET ME HAVE MY PORRIDGE AND I
DON'T KNOW WHAT ELSE!"* said the horrible voice,
and the yellow tongue came right to the serpent's lips and
Harry saw, with a sensation of relief which is impossible
to describe, that it wasn't a tongue at all, only Big George
in his yellow rain slicker, and that it wasn't really a sea
serpent's head, but just a big, wooden, floating fake with

orange Chinese lanterns for eyes and white fence pickets for teeth!

"Oh, my gracious," said Harry. "Oh, my goodness, Big George, you have frightened me something fierce!"

"I'm sorry," said the enormous bear, and he really did sound truly apologetic. "But Little George made me do it all in order to help the gollops!"

There was a splashing in the water around the bend of the cave leading to the entrance and a nervous voice called out, "Harry? Are you there, Harry? Are you alright?"

"Yes, Fred," Harry called back, recognizing the voice and the nervousness at once. "I think everything's going to be fine now."

thirteen Everybody Has a Party

The Commodore invited everyone to dinner on board the *Jo-Anne-Mae* that night back in the harbor at Beartown-on-the-Sea, even Big George, and it was because of him they served the food on deck, since the enormous bear was unable to get through the hatches leading below.

Before eating, of course, all the bears sang the Bearmanian National Sea Chanty. Harry and Fred had made it their business to learn the words and sang them proudly, feeling like two regular salts. Big and Little George mumbled gamely through the parts they didn't know, and the Hermit hummed through it all cheerfully and with great enthusiasm:

"Where e'er you sail,
Bearmania,
We'll sail along with you;
We'll never fail
Bearmania,
Ne'er wail upon the blue!"

Then Sailor Ned served the dinner and it was obvious
he had excelled himself, everything was so good and so
juicy. There were steamed lobsters and corn on the cob
with lots of butter and some sort of delicious corn bread,
and for dessert there was the best lemon meringue pie
Harry had ever eaten with absolutely the biggest, fluffiest
top on it he had ever seen. Everybody ate it all with the
greatest enjoyment, even Little George, though the sight
of the tiny bear's usually sour face beaming smiles was a
trifle startling.

After dinner the Hermit helped Ned with the dishes—
it seemed the shaggy old bear was seriously thinking of
joining the Navy—while the other bears chatted over
cocoa with a spoonful of whipped cream in each cup.

"I came across the gollops three years ago," said Little
George, "hiding amidst the rocks of Wrecked Bear Reef.
There were only four of them, then, and they were small
and pitiful and scared and hungry. I didn't know where
they came from, nor what they were, but I could see they
needed help bad, so I called them gollops and took them
back to the island."

"But they wouldn't eat anything," said Big George,
shaking his head sadly.

*The shaggy old bear was
thinking of joining the Navy.*

"No, they wouldn't eat a cussed thing," said Little
George. "We tried all the usual stuff you'd figure a sea
critter would go for, but no luck, so then we tried them
on what you or I might like."

"We tried flapjacks with maple syrup on them," said Big George, licking his lips at the memory, "but they wouldn't touch them so I had to eat all we cooked and the syrup, too."

"I had to eat all we cooked and the syrup, too."

"All the time they were getting pitifuller and pitifuller," continued Little George, "and I just didn't know what to do. These gollops were the first things I had been able to like for I don't know how long. I'd gotten real fond of them, don't you see? And now they were dying on me."

The tiny bear shook his head sadly, then he smiled.

"But one day I was walking them along the shore when we came across a clump of sea tulips, which had drifted in from the mainland, and the gollops made those little woofs they make, and they sailed right into them and ate them up, every last one!"

"So Little George had me row to the mainland and get as many sea tulips as I could stuff in the boat, and I brought them back and we started the flower farm in the cave," said Big George, proudly.

"They thrived and were happy," said Little George. "But soon there were more of them and I got to worrying about someone finding them in the cave and doing them harm. I have a very suspicious nature, you see, being so small, and me and my brother on our own since we were cubs."

"So Little George thought up the sea serpent," said his brother with a bright smile.

"They liked to follow Big George as he rowed," said Little George, "and it struck me you could take them for one animal, strung out behind him like that, so I made the rowboat look like the serpent's head, and it worked."

"You kept the gollops safe out on the reef during the day," said Harry, "and at night Big George would lead them to the cove to meet you, and then to the cave."

"Unless you turned the lighthouse signal from green to red as a warning" observed Professor Waldo, "as we saw you do."

"That's all there was to it," said Little George.

"Well, I certainly wish you had trusted us all more," said the Commodore, sighing. "We could have had the gollops clearing our harbors of sea tulips years ago, as they will now under your command as Official Gollop Chief, Little George. Too, not having all this fuss about a monster would have saved us an awful lot of trouble!"

"Oh, I don't know," mused Professor Waldo. "I enjoyed the idea of hunting a sea serpent. And so did you, Commodore. Admit it."

"Well," growled the old salt, tugging at a brass button, "it *was* kind of fun."

"Without this happening," observed Professor Waldo,

"I might never have come to perfect my suction climber, nor my water motor. Though my flexible lens camera still does need work."

But the best comment came from the old Hermit Bear, who had just come up from the galley with Sailor Ned.

"If all this hadn't happened I'd still be wasting my time being all alone," he said. "It's much more fun with other bears around!"

Harry smiled. "It is, isn't it?" said the fat bear spy.

And they all strolled over to the railing of the *Jo-Anne-Mae* to watch the gollops playing below in the sea tulips.

Gahan Wilson was born in Evanston, Illinois, and graduated from The Art Institute of Chicago. He later attended the Académie Julian in Paris. He is the author/illustrator of *Harry, the Fat Bear Spy* and *The Bang Bang Family*, and has illustrated many other children's books—among them *The Future of Hooper Toote* by Felice Holman. His cartoons and drawings appear regularly in *Punch, Playboy, Audubon, The New York Times,* and *The National Lampoon.* There have been several collections of his cartoons, *I Paint What I See* and *The Cracked Cosmos of Gahan Wilson,* as well as a collection of his short stories. He presently has a syndicated newspaper comic page, *Gahan Wilson's Sunday Comics.* He lives in New York City.